The Little Blue Digger and the Very Muddy Day

MORGANTOWN PUBLIC LIBRARY
373 SPRUCE STREET
MORGANTOWN, WV 26505

by Harriet Tuppen

illustrated by Branislav Gapic

D1385398

For free printable colouring pages of Little Blue and his friends, visit:

www.tuppenbooks.com/fun/

© 2016 Harriet Tuppen

All rights reserved. No part of this book may be used or reproduced in any manner without written permission from the author, except in the case of brief excerpts used in critical articles or reviews. For information regarding permission, please contact the author at tuppenbooks@gmail.com.

ISBN-13: 978-1535074636
ISBN-10: 1535074639

For Henry

It had been a
VERY rainy week in
Builders Town.

The construction site was a big muddy mess!
Little Blue and his friends were having a great time
splashing through the puddles as they worked.

Only Wide Red was out of sorts. He loved his shiny red paint and didn't like getting it muddy.

All of a sudden, the team heard clanking and sputtering. It was Old Rusty! "I need help at the farm!" wheezed the tractor. "The sheep are in trouble!"

"Let's go!" said Big Yellow. The friends raced through the wet countryside as the rain began to clear.

They got to the farm. The field was a muddy lake and the poor sheep were stranded in the middle!

HELP

Little Blue thought hard.
"Wide Red, come with me!" he said,
heading towards the water.

Wide Red looked at all the mud. His lovely red paint would be a terrible mess! But the sheep needed his help, so he plunged in.

HELP

The brave pair reached the island. Little Blue carefully lifted the sheep onto Wide Red's back.

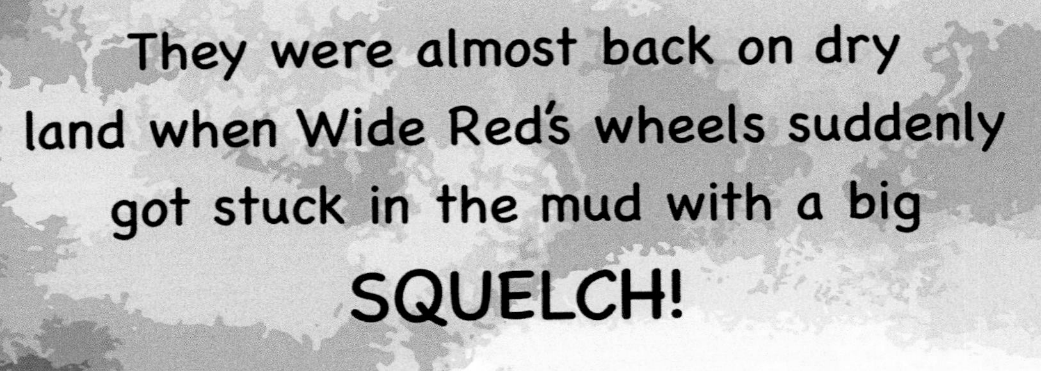

They were almost back on dry land when Wide Red's wheels suddenly got stuck in the mud with a big

SQUELCH!

Oh no! What now?

Tall Orange quickly rolled forward.
She lowered her long boom across the water.
Soon all of the sheep were safe.

Then Strong Green towed
Wide Red clear of the mud.
He really wasn't very
red any more!

But the mucky truck didn't mind.

"The sheep
are safe. And
look! The rain will
soon clean me up!"
he laughed.

And indeed it did ...
with a little help from
some new friends!

The End

MORGANTOWN PUBLIC LIBRARY
373 SPRUCE STREET
MORGANTOWN, WV 26505

45591641R00020

Made in the USA
San Bernardino, CA
30 July 2019